Bintou's Braids

To my mother, Marcelle Diouf, who filled my childhood with music, stories and books.—S.D.

Thank you, God. Dedicated to the people of the Olorun Foundation and Ouagadougou, Burkina Faso, West Africa, for sharing the spirit of life, art and creation.—S.E.

Book design by Carrie Leeb, Leeb & Sons.
Typeset in Weiss Bold.
The illustrations in this book were rendered in oil paint.
Printed in Hong Kong.

Library of Congress Cataloging-in-Publication Data
Diouf, Sylviane.
Bintou's braids / by Sylviane A. Diouf ; illustrated by Shane W. Evans.
p. cm.
Summary: When Bintou, a little girl living in West Africa,
finally gets her wish for braids, she discovers that what she
dreamed for has been hers all along.
ISBN 0-8118-2514-0
[1. Braids (Hairdressing)--Fiction. 2. Hair—Fiction. 3. Africa, West—Fiction.]
I. Evans, Shane, ill. II. Title.
PZ7.D6218 Bi 2000
[E]--dc21   99-050820

Distributed in Canada by Raincoast Books
9050 Shaughnessy Street, Vancouver, British Columbia V6P 6E5

10 9 8 7 6 5 4 3 2 1

Chronicle Books LLC
85 Second Street, San Francisco, California 94105

www.chroniclebooks.com/Kids

Bintou's Braids

by Sylviane A. Diouf

illustrated by Shane W. Evans

chronicle books·san francisco

My name is Bintou and I want braids.

My hair is short and fuzzy. My hair is plain and silly.
All I have is four little tufts on my head.

Sometimes, I dream that little birds make their nest in my hair. It would be such a nice place for babies to rest. There, they would sleep and they would sing. But most of the time, I dream of braids. Long braids with gold coins and seashells.

My sister Fatou has braids and she looks pretty. When she bends over me, the beads in her braids touch my cheek. She asks, "Bintou, why are you crying?" I say, "I want to be pretty like you." She says, "Little girls can't have braids. Tomorrow I'll cornrow your hair." That's all I ever get—cornrows.

This morning, Grandma Soukeye is coming to our village for the baptism of my baby brother who is eight days old. Mommy has sent me to meet her. Here she is now, in her blue gown.

Grandma Soukeye knows everything. That's what my mother says. She says old people know so much because they have lived such a long time and have learned more than anybody else. Since Grandma knows everything, I ask her why little girls can't have braids.

"A long time ago, there was a young girl named Coumba who thought only about how pretty she was," she says while stroking my head. "Everyone envied her and Coumba became vain and selfish. It was then that the mothers decided that little girls would not be allowed to have braids, so that they would only make friends, play and learn. From then on, Coumba got cornrows."

Grandma pulls gently on my ear and says, "Now, little Bintou, when you're older, it's fine to want to look your best and show everybody that you have become a young woman. But you are still just a girl. You will get braids when it is time."

When I sleep that night, I dream that I'm old. I dream that I'm sixteen and I have braids with gold coins and seashells. And when I turn my head, the sun follows me. I shine like a queen.

When I wake up, I look into the mirror. But I am still Bintou, with four little tufts on my head.

Today, our yard is full of people in their best clothes. Earlier, Aunt Safi shaved my baby brother's head and now she holds him for all to see. Daddy whispers the name he and Mommy have chosen to Serigne Mansour, the elder who leads the prayer. Serigne Mansour murmurs a short prayer in the baby's ears and then he says, aloud, "His name is Abdou."

Now, we can eat and have fun. Huge platters of lamb and rice appear. I look for the fish balls in hot sauce that burn my tongue. I eat sugary fritters and papayas.

I watch the women from behind the mango tree. My sister Fatou is there. She has put perfumed oil on her scalp, between her braids, to make it shine. And also, she says, so that the skin pulled so tight hurts less.

Mommy's friends have braids with gold coins on their forehead. They say it is to show us children how the great-grandmothers we never knew wore their hair.

It took three days to finish Aunt Aida's braids. There are so many that even my older sister Maty could not count them all.

Mariama, who studies in the city, and her friend have braids that reach down to their waists. Her friend is not from here. I can tell because she talks with an accent. When I gave her a papaya, she said, "I'm Terry and I come from America." I asked if the little girls there have braids. "Many do. And they put colorful barrettes on each braid." They must look pretty, the little girls in her country!

The women laugh and shake their heads, and the beads on their braids sound like rain. All I have is four little tufts of hair on my head and I am sad.

I walk to the beach like I always do when I want to be alone. It is so quiet, I only hear the waves, the wind in the palm trees and the birds. And then, screams. When I look up, I see two boys waving and shouting. Their canoe is sinking. I have to get the fishermen, quick, quick.

The path to the village is wide and easy, but it will be faster if I take the shortcut through the bush. Nobody uses it because there are long thorns and sharp stones. I run and jump as fast as I can.

"Bouba and Yaya are drowning!" I cry when I reach the clearing. The fishermen rush past me and push a canoe to the water. Their paddles move fast, fast, fast. They throw a rope to the boys and pull them in.

Back in the village, everyone gathers around me. Aunt Alimatou, Bouba and Yaya's mother, brings me biscuits. Mommy says, "You are a smart little girl. If you had taken the good path, you would have arrived too late. You have saved these boys' lives. We shall reward you. Tell us what you would like."

Before I can speak, Fatou says, "She wants braids." Mommy runs her fingers through my hair where only two tufts remain. The thread around the others broke when I ran through the bush. "Then braids you shall have."

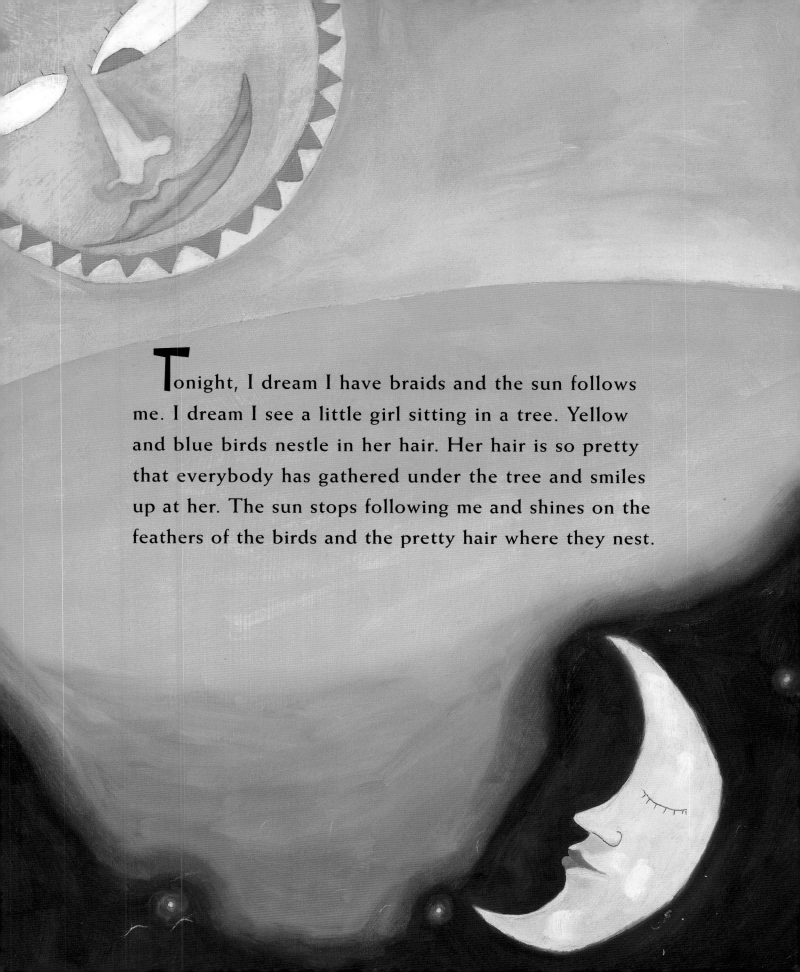

Tonight, I dream I have braids and the sun follows me. I dream I see a little girl sitting in a tree. Yellow and blue birds nestle in her hair. Her hair is so pretty that everybody has gathered under the tree and smiles up at her. The sun stops following me and shines on the feathers of the birds and the pretty hair where they nest.

In the morning, Grandma Soukeye calls me to her room. She tells me to sit on the floor between her legs. She rubs perfumed oil in my hair. "You're a special little girl," she whispers. "Your hair will be special too." I tell her that Aunt Awa is coming to braid my hair. But she says, "Hush, now." I feel her fingers, fast and light. I think she's doing cornrows. I feel tears in my eyes. I shut them tight. When it's over, I don't want to look in the mirror she holds.

Grandma says, "Open your eyes, little Bintou." And that's when I see yellow and blue birds in my hair. Gone is the plain girl with the four tufts on her head. In the mirror is a girl with pretty hair looking back at me.

I am Bintou. My hair is black and shiny. My hair is soft and pretty. I am the girl with birds in her hair. The sun follows me and I'm happy.